Does God Know How to Tie Shoes?

By NANCY WHITE CARLSTROM

Illustrated by LORI McELRATH-ESLICK

WILLIAM B. EERDMANS PUBLISHING COMPANY • GRAND RAPIDS, MICHIGAN

Text copyright © 1993 by Nancy White Carlstrom
Illustrations copyright © 1993 by Lori McElrath-Eslick

Published 1993 by Eerdmans Books for Young Readers
an imprint of Wm. B. Eerdmans Publishing Co.
255 Jefferson Ave. S.E., Grand Rapids, Michigan 49503
P.O. Box 163, Cambridge CB3 9PU U.K.

Printed in Singapore

03   02   01   00   15   14   13   12

Spring Arbor Edition

Library of Congress Cataloging-in-Publication Data

Carlstrom, Nancy White.
   Does God know how to tie shoes? / Nancy White Carlstrom;
illustrated by Lori McElrath-Eslick.
   1 v. (unpaged) : col. ill. ; 24 x 26 cm.
   Includes Scripture references from the Psalms.
   Summary: As a young girl walks with her parents through the countryside,
her questions elicit responses that help her to know God better.
ISBN 0-8028-5074-X (cloth: alk. paper)
ISBN 0-8028-5125-8 (pbk.: alk. paper)
   [1. God — Fiction.   2. Parent and child — Fiction.]
I. McElrath-Eslick, Lori, ill.   II. Title.
PZ7.C21684Do   1993
[E] — dc20   94-136880
                                         AC

Illustration of cow closeup courtesy of Robert W. Harper from *Ladybug Magazine,*
October 1991, Volume 2, Number 2; © 1991 by Lori McElrath-Eslick.

For Mom and Dad,
who nurtured my faith
with love and thanks.

N.W.C.

To Golman and Camille,
God knows I love you.

L.M.E.

Mama, what does God wear?

I don't know, Katrina. But He dresses the hills with joy and the meadows with sheep. And the flowers never have to worry about what to put on.

I think God wears orange beads when the sun comes up and a big grey hat when it rains.

Does God know how to tie
shoes, Papa?

By His word the heavens and
earth were made. He breathed
and the stars took their place.

Then God must know how to
tie shoes.

Mama, how does God talk?

Sometimes He whispers in a still,
small voice. Like when you hold
a seashell to your ear. Sometimes
He roars over the water and His
glory thunders.

Like a lion, Mama?

Yes, a great, kind lion.

Does God have wings, Papa?

God wraps His love around us
like the wings of a mother hen
protecting her baby chicks. And
He knows how all the birds fly.

God probably loves crows too!

Mama, does God get cold and hungry?

Well, He feels sad when people are cold and hungry.

God must shiver when He sees Old Joe in his torn coat. When it snows, I will give him my mittens.

Does God ever cry, Papa?

Yes, I think He does.

Because of the cold, hungry
people?

Yes, and when people can't live
together without fighting.

And when Thomas pulls Sara's
hair. It's so long she can sit on it.

Mama, does God have any pets?

The animals and birds of the forest are his, and every cow on a thousand hills.

Maybe God would like us to get a puppy!

Does God ever sing, Papa?

Probably. He rejoices with the fields and sings with the trees while the rivers clap.

I think I see God riding on a cloud. That makes me sing!

Mama, is God sad when He
doesn't get a letter?

God does like to hear from us,
Katrina. We call that prayer.
It can be a way of talking . . .
or singing . . .

. . . or playing my drum!

Does God like to paint, Papa?

He paints the sunrise and sunset,
and spreads out the heavens like
a cloth.

I bet He likes painting rainbows
best of all. Just like me.

Mama, does God ever have to
clean up His room?

He wakes the dawn and makes
sure the seasons change. Yes, He
keeps everything in order.

But even in His closet?

Does God go to sleep, Papa?

No, Katrina. God never sleeps.

But doesn't He ever get tired?

Well, He did rest after making this world.

But Mama, where in the world is God now?

God is here when we talk together.
He's with you when you feel happy
and when you feel sad.

And scared too?

Yes, when you are scared, He is there.
God is always with you.

Papa, does God know my name?

Oh yes, and the stars in the heavens too.

Goodnight, Mama. Goodnight, Papa. Goodnight, God.

I'm Katrina with a K!

Scripture References from the Psalms

Psalm 104:1-2a O LORD my God, you are very great;
you are clothed with splendor and majesty.
He wraps himself in light as with a garment.

Psalm 65:12b-13 The hills are clothed with gladness.
The meadows are covered with flocks
and the valleys are mantled with grain;
they shout for joy and sing.

Psalm 33:6 By the word of the LORD were the heavens made,
their starry host by the breath of his mouth.

Psalm 29:3-4 The voice of the LORD is over the waters;
the God of glory thunders,
the LORD thunders over the mighty waters.
The voice of the LORD is powerful;
the voice of the LORD is majestic.

Psalm 50:11 I know every bird in the mountains,
and the creatures of the field are mine.

Psalm 91:4 He will cover you with his feathers,
and under his wings you will find refuge.

Psalm 72:12-13a For he will deliver the needy who cry out,
the afflicted who have no one to help.
He will take pity on the weak and the needy.

Psalm 85:10 Love and faithfulness meet together;
righteousness and peace kiss each other.

Psalm 50:10 For every animal of the forest is mine,
and the cattle on a thousand hills.

Psalm 96:12 Let the fields be jubilant, and everything in them.
Then all the trees of the forest will sing for joy.

Psalm 68:4   Sing to God, sing praise to his name,
             extol him who rides on the clouds —
             his name is the LORD —
             and rejoice before him.

Psalm 100:2, 4b   Worship the LORD with gladness;
             come before him with joyful songs.
             Give thanks to him and praise his name.

Psalm 150:3-6   Praise him with the sounding of the trumpet,
             praise him with the harp and lyre,
             praise him with tambourine and dancing,
             praise him with the strings and flute,
             praise him with the clash of cymbals,
             praise him with resounding cymbals.
             Let everything that has breath praise the LORD.

Psalm 50:1   The Mighty One, God, the LORD,
             speaks and summons the earth
             from the rising of the sun to the place where it sets.

Psalm 104:19   The moon marks off the seasons,
             and the sun knows when to go down.

Psalm 139:9   If I rise on the wings of the dawn,
             if I settle on the far side of the sea,
             even there your hand will guide me,
             your right hand will hold me fast.

Psalm 145:18   The LORD is near to all who call on him,
             to all who call on him in truth.

Psalm 147:4-5   He determines the number of the stars
             and calls them each by name.
             Great is our LORD and mighty in power;
             his understanding has no limit.

*From the New
International Version*